Dev's Christmas

Dev's Christmas

Keith Salisbury

Black Lyon Publishing, LLC

DEV'S CHRISTMAS
Copyright © 2010 by KEITH SALISBURY

Our books may be ordered through your local bookstore or by visiting the publisher:

www.BlackLyonPublishing.com

Black Lyon Publishing, LLC
PO Box 567
Baker City, OR 97814

This is a work of fiction. All of the characters, names, events, organizations and conversations in this novel are either the products of the author's vivid imagination or are used in a fictitious way for the purposes of this story.

ISBN-10:   1-934912-33-6
ISBN-13:   978-1-934912-33-1

Written, published and printed in
the United States of America.

Black Lyon Publishing
Lyonettes
Contemporary Romance

*This novella is dedicated to my parents,
who taught me the value of reading and writing,
and the joys of a family Christmas;
and to my wife, Jodi, for putting up with an
eccentric writer for nearly a quarter of a century,
and teaching him about love and commitment along the way.*

NE

Thursday, December 22

It had all seemed so easy a week ago, Devlin Walker thought as he herded his black Chrysler two-door along the expressway. Snow swirled across the pavement in the oval glow of the headlights and charged at the windshield.

He looked over at Nadine Trent in the passenger seat, huddled deep in her violet down coat, a multi-colored knit hat perched atop her head, long dark hair spilling about her oval face. He caught her eye, and she smiled at him. He could tell she was nervous, but he wasn't sure if it was because of the weather or because they were on their way to her parents' home for the Christmas holiday. The Bing Crosby CD in the stereo gave the whole trip a surreal feeling, but he'd been a fan since he was a kid. As his eyes checked the road behind them in the rearview mirror, he paused for a glance at her six-year-old daughter, Molly, in the backseat, half asleep but looking out the side window at the lights and decorations they passed in the night. It was a long journey from their college town north to Nadine's mid-Michigan home, over two and a half hours in the best of conditions. They had picked up the snow about an hour into the trip, and he knew for a little girl on a holiday trip three days before Christmas, the ride must seem like it was taking forever. But she had been good most of the way, talking occasionally but so far not asking the dreaded question: "Are we there yet?"

As he turned his attention back to the road before them, he marveled that the whole trip had begun with a simple request. The week before, knowing she would be embarking on a major journey, Nadine had asked him to check out her ten-year-old Ford to make sure it would be up to the trip. They lived in the same Depression-era six-unit, three-story apartment building—he on the top floor, she and Molly on the second— and occasionally their paths crossed on campus where they were both working on master's degrees, so it was only natural they had become friends.

The news about the car wasn't good, however.

"How bad is it?" she had asked, as they stood in the parking area next to it.

"Well, to be honest I wouldn't drive the old girl across town, let alone three hours up into those boondocks you call home," he had said. "The tires are shot, and she's chugging oil like a frat boy drinks beer at a kegger. If she was a dog, you'd have had her put to sleep by now."

"So you're saying I shouldn't take her on the trip."

"Not unless you want to soak some money into her, or have a strong desire to do some walking."

"How much would it take to get her ready, do you think?" she asked.

He had rubbed his chin to allow himself another moment or two for thought. A hundred dollars or a thousand, he knew with Christmas a week away that she didn't have any extra money. Things were generally tight for the two of them even during the good times.

"At a bare minimum, it'll take a couple of hundred for tires," he had said. "Work on that engine will get pricey, and that's if we could find a mechanic who could get it done in the next couple of days. Which is doubtful."

"Oh," she'd said, her body sagging with the weight of her world.

And it was at that point the whole thing got complicated.

"Look, if you're really set on going, I'll run you two up there and then pick you up when you're ready to come back," he had said.

"That's crazy," she had replied, shaking her head. "Why would you drive that far out of your way, just to get us home for Christmas?"

He had shrugged. "I don't really have anything else to do and the trip is really important to you. I'll probably be heading north anyway to go skiing, so it's on the way."

"I thought you and Sara were going to Chicago for Christmas."

Dev shook his head. "Nadine, honey, you are so out of the loop. Sara and I got into a huge fight over a week ago. She's not even speaking to me. I think a trip anywhere with her is out of the question."

"Oh," she had said. "I'm sorry. Guess I have been pretty much wrapped up in my own problems, with school and the holidays. Are you doing okay?"

"Me? I'm fine. We weren't all that serious anyway." Even as he had said it, he had known there was more truth to that thought than he cared to admit. Sara had been right, no matter how hard he might try to deny it.

"This is our exit," she said, pulling him out of his thoughts and back to the task at hand.

Out of the darkness and swirling snow the big green exit sign loomed closer. Devlin switched on his right turn blinker out of habit, even though there were no other cars around, slowed the car and eased it off of the highway and onto the exit ramp. He slowed the car more and at the bottom of the ramp came to a stop.

"Right?" he asked.

"And then left where the road ends, and right again at the next light," Nadine replied.

He nodded. "Okay."

It was darker on the two-lane, and the snow on the road

was thicker. He switched on his brights, but with the swirling snow, they were less than helpful so he switched back.

Indicating the cell phone resting in one of the cup holders, he said, "You probably should call your folks, let them know where we are."

Nadine nodded, picked up the phone and put through the call. As she talked to her mother, his thoughts returned again to the previous week, and another phone call and its affect on the journey.

It was the morning after their conversation about her car and the trip north. It was a Thursday, and they both had morning classes so were car-pooling in the Chrysler. They had already dropped Molly off at school.

"I talked to my mom last night and let her know we were coming home for Christmas," she had said.

"Yeah?" had been his non-committal reply.

"She said if you don't really have plans, you're welcome to stay at the house with us."

"That's nice of her, but not necessary. I'm a big boy now, and I'm used to being on my own for the holidays."

The conversation had continued after he parked the car in one of the big multi-level garages, and they were walking across campus to University Hall, where she had an office as a graduate assistant in the English Department.

"You don't understand my mother," she said. "Family is important to her, and she believes that families should be together for the holidays. Especially Christmas."

He had shrugged. "Well, I can understand that, I guess. But I'm not part of the family. I'm just a friend."

"I guess Molly and I talk about you so much, Mom considers you part of our family," had been Nadine's reply. "You're family as far as Molly's concerned, 'Uncle Dev.' Besides, what would you do otherwise? Go up to some ski resort and sit around for a few days checking out the snow bunnies?"

He had grinned at that. "That does sound like a good idea. I'm just not sure about all this family-for-the-holiday business.

That wasn't part of my childhood, you know."

"I know. But you could try it this once. For Molly and me."

And that was the argument that had done him in. He had always had difficulty deny the two of them anything it was in his power to provide.

🎁

"Mom said she's got some vegetable soup staying warm on the stove," Nadine said, pulling him once again from his reverie. "And she says to be careful and not to hurry."

"Careful's my middle name."

"And here all this time I thought it was Wayne."

He risked a quick glance at her and was pleased to see the smile on her face—the same one she used to light up a room on rare occasions. She had been in a constant state of worry since before Thanksgiving, and it was good to see her relax and enjoy the moment.

The two-lane highway was dark with not much traffic. Most of the houses had mercury lights in their yards, and many had Christmas lights and decorations up. The swirling snow made the older farm houses and barns they passed look like Christmas card paintings. It was all vastly different from the urban and suburban landscape he had grown up in. His was a world of carefully coiffed lawns, subdued landscape lighting and out-buildings hidden behind houses. He found himself wishing the snow would let up so he could concentrate less on the driving and more on enjoying the passing scenery. He was beginning to understand, at least in part, what drew Nadine back to her roots.

Within an hour they were parking his car in her parents' driveway, up by the house. Nadine got out on her side, gathering her purse and Molly's backpack from the backseat. Dev got out on his side, pushed his seat forward and roused Molly from her half-sleep. By the time they were all out of the car and turned toward the house, the back door of the twenty-year-old farmhouse had opened and people were spilling out.

Nadine's mother led the way, and Molly burst from the car

running toward her grandmother. Mrs. Trent was an older version of Nadine, her hair not as dark mixed with gray, nor as long. Even with the few wrinkles, he could easily see where his friend got her looks and that twinkle in her green eyes. Mrs. Trent was dressed in dark knit slacks and a green sweatshirt with a Christmas pattern on the front.

Next in line was Nadine's younger sister, Ronnie, another copy of their mother, though not as tall. She wore tight faded blue jeans and a maroon sweater.

Nadine's father stood on the porch, a barrel-chested man with graying dark hair and deep lines in his face. He was dressed in green work pants with suspenders and a brown flannel shirt. He motioned behind him to Shane, Nadine's teen-aged brother and said, "Give 'em a hand with the luggage, boy."

Shane was a farm kid with dark curly hair and a large smile. He wore battered jeans and a Detroit Lions sweatshirt, and came out into the snow with his boots unlaced.

While Nadine and Molly passed out and collected hugs, Dev popped the latch on the trunk and went around to the back of the car. Shane met him there as Dev was scooping up suitcases and duffle bags. He said to the younger boy, "Let's leave the presents till last. I don't think there's anything that will freeze."

Shane nodded and they headed to the porch with the armfuls of gear.

"Now you boys just set that stuff inside the door and we'll move it inside," Mrs. Trent said. "No sense in tracking snow all through the house. And when you're done we'll get you kids something to eat, get you warmed up."

"Yes, ma'am," Dev replied as he deposited his load and headed back to the car.

"That sounds great, Mom," Shane said. "I'm starving."

"Starving! You've been doing nothing but eat since you got home this afternoon," she replied.

"That's not true. I did chores before supper, and just a little while ago I plowed the driveway and shoveled the porch."

Dev shook his head, enjoying the good-natured ribbing, so different from the way he grew up. He gathered up another armful of luggage and headed again to the door.

After the luggage and Christmas packages had been put away and the travelers had eaten, the family gathered in the living room to catch up and relax. Mrs. Trent had tucked herself into her easy chair with a quilt draped over her legs. Mr. Trent settled into his easy chair as well. Dev sat on the sofa, Molly asleep in his lap, while Nadine rested with her back against his side. Her sister sat at the other end of the sofa. Her brother was stretched out on the floor in front of the Christmas tree. It came as no surprise to Dev that the tree had been alive just a day or two before, given the large acreage of woods behind the farmhouse. He enjoyed its pungent spruce aroma, which mingled with the wood smoke from the furnace and the cooking smells from the kitchen. He smiled as he thought, *This is what a home should smell like at Christmas.*

"Well, Devlin, we certainly are grateful to you for bringing the girls home for Christmas," Mrs. Trent said. "And we're glad you agreed to spend the holiday with us, but we were surprised to hear you didn't have plans with your family."

"Mother!" Nadine said as she sat forward on the sofa.

"It's okay, honey." He turned his attention to Mrs. Trent. "Like I told Nadine last week, I appreciate the invitation, but it wasn't necessary. Getting together for Christmas has never been big in my family."

"You mean you don't get together with your parents even for the day?" Mrs. Trent replied.

Dev smiled. "That would be kind of difficult, not to mention uncomfortable. My parents got divorced shortly after I graduated from high school. Mother's out in California with her new husband. Dad's still in town, but he married a younger woman. They have two little kids and having the older son from the previous marriage around is kind of awkward."

"Oh, I'm so sorry."

"Don't be," Dev said. "We never really did the whole Christmas thing even when I was a kid. Dad's an engineer and he's got a pretty good job. My mother's parents were quite well to do, so even when I was little, Mother wasn't very domestic. We had a live-in nanny/housekeeper/cook. An older lady. She was great. But she always took time off around Christmas and Mother certainly wasn't going to cook or clean up from any holiday nonsense. When I was little, we either went to Grandpa and Grandma Walker's, or to Grandfather and Grandmother Kendrall's for the holidays. Then as I got older, we started going to Disney World or Mexico, or on a cruise."

Shane sat up on one elbow. "Disney World? For Christmas? That would be so cool."

Dev nodded. "Yeah, the first couple of times were cool. But it got old, fast. After a couple of years, it was just like any other time at Disney World just with more people."

"Are any of your grandparents still alive?" asked Mr. Trent.

"They all are. Grandpa and Grandma Walker have a farm about an hour west of town. They're pretty much retired, but they still live at the old homestead. My uncle runs the farm, with his kids. I've gone there a couple of times, but I'm sort of a fifth wheel."

"And you aren't welcome with either of your parents?" Mrs. Trent asked, the concern evident in her voice.

"Oh sure. I could spend the holidays with Dad and Stephanie and the kids," Dev said. "We get along great and I'm more than welcome there. But I always feel I'm in the way, so I usually go over before or after Christmas, take the kids their presents, have dinner, that sort of thing. And usually sometime in December Dad and I go out for supper, just the two of us."

"What about your mother?"

"Well, like I said, she's out in California now. She married an older guy, who's probably almost as rich as Grandfather, so she's quite happy. They do the whole Palm Springs society thing for Christmas, which is about as much fun as having multiple root canals done on the same day. What can I say? I'm my father's son."

Mrs. Trent nodded. "Then this year we'll just have to make sure you have a special family Christmas. And no arguments. It's not polite to argue with your hostess."

Nadine turned to look up at Dev. "See? I told you." Then she turned back to her mother. "And I think it's time a certain little princess got put to bed. Who's sleeping where, Mom?"

"Well, I thought we'd put you and Molly in your old room. Verona gets her old room, and we'll put Devlin in Shane's room. Shane can sleep on the sofa."

As Nadine stood up and took Molly from his arms, Dev said to Mrs. Trent, "If it's all the same to you folks, I'd just as soon sleep on the sofa and let Shane have his room. As Nadine can tell you, I only sleep about four hours a night, and when I do sleep, I can literally sleep anywhere. Being in the living room won't bother me, and I'll be awake at the crack of dawn anyway."

"Are you sure?" Mrs. Trent replied. "It's just not good manners to make the company sleep on the sofa."

He smiled as he stood up. "But you're not making me, I'm asking to. There's a difference. And besides, Nadine's already explained to me that I'm considered family. So there should be no problem, right?"

Mrs. Trent shook her head in resignation. "Okay, if you're sure you wouldn't be more comfortable in a room."

"Word of honor, I'll be perfectly fine out here." That settled, he took Molly from Nadine, the child never fully awakening in either transfer, and said, "Lead the way and we'll get this little monkey to bed."

🎁

The lights in the living room were out, except for the table lamp by the sofa. Dev had the sleeper sofa opened and made up, but he sat at the base of the mattress with his back resting against the back of the sofa. He wore gray sweatpants and a gray T-shirt with the university's logo on it for his sleepwear. A hardback book was laying upside down and open on the mattress next to him. He had been reading *A Christmas Carol* by Charles Dickens, but had only gotten through the first stave and the arrival of Marley's ghost. His concentration had been hauled away from the book by his surroundings—the quiet of the room, but for the small creaks and settlings of the house, the good food smells drifting in from the kitchen, and the freshness of the blue spruce standing in the corner. The whole experience had been much more than he had expected. Even in the short time he had been in the home, he was already beginning to feel like a member of the family, and that was not a feeling he was used to or comfortable with. Hearing the closeness in Nadine's voice as she talked about her parents, sister and brother was one thing, but to see it in person was almost overwhelming. He was a lone wolf, always had been, and running with a pack was disconcerting.

The sound of footsteps brought him out of his reverie. He looked up to see Nadine coming across the living room toward him. Her long flannel nightgown billowed around her as she walked, and he could almost believe she was the Ghost of Christmas Present coming to take him away on an adventure. Dev shook his head and smiled.

"You're up kind of late, aren't you?" he asked.

Nadine sat down on the edge of the bed portion of the sleeper sofa. "Just wanted to make sure you were okay down here before I give up for the night. You comfortable?"

"Sure. Just doing a little light reading before I catch a few zees."

Nadine picked up his book, careful not to lose his place. As she looked at the title she raised an eyebrow. "*A Christmas Carol*? I never would have expected it from you."

Dev shrugged. "You caught me in a moment of sentimentality. It's one of my few Christmas traditions. I first read it in high school over Christmas break. I don't think I've missed a Christmas since. It's like spending the holiday with an old friend."

"Or a member of the family?"

"Ooh, and I thought you were an English major, not a psych student."

"An understanding of psychology is very helpful to an understanding of literature and writers. Why they write what they write. That sort of thing."

"Yeah, well, mine was always history and fine art. Whatever her ulterior motives, Mother made sure I had a good background in art and style."

"She did a good job," Nadine said in agreement. "Thank you, again, for bringing us up here today. And I'm glad you're staying through the holiday with us. You've gotten to be such an important part of our lives, I can't imagine spending Christmas without you around. And I know Molly can't either."

"You know I always like spending time with my two favorite girls."

She nodded. "I know. And I hope all this family stuff doesn't get too much for you. I know you're not used to it."

"It's different, but so far it's been fun and interesting too. I'll be fine."

Nadine stood up. "Well, I guess I'd better get off to bed. See you in the morning, Dev."

"Goodnight, Nadine. And don't worry, it's going to be a great weekend."

He watched her leave the room, then let out a large exhale before picking up his book again.

WO

Friday, December 23

Dev was up early the next morning and had the sleeper sofa stored away before Mr. Trent had the coffee on. After coffee and a leisurely breakfast with his hosts, he retired to the living room and the sofa with his book in order to stay out of the way. But he soon tired of reading, and before the late risers had finished with their breakfasts, he was dressed in his jeans and flannel shirt, bundled up for the cold, and headed outside to see what he could find to do.

The winter morning air was crisp and clear and bit into Dev's lungs with a sharpness he enjoyed. The dampness of the air brought out the sweet tang of the wood smoke from the farmhouse stove. The fresh snow crunched under his boots as he walked out the back door toward the rear portion of the farm. The crispness of the air made him glad he had brought along a ski coat as well as his winter dress coat. He had remembered what winter on a farm could be like and had come prepared.

Shane had the family's larger Farmall tractor fired up and was plowing the driveway again, using the drag blade with the three-point hitch on the back. He waved at Dev as the visitor trudged through the snow, but quickly returned his attention to his plowing. Back at the end of the drive where the outbuildings were, Mr. Trent was tossing wood into a battered wooden wagon bed hitched to the smaller Farmall. The wagon was backed up to a lean-to stacked rafter-high with cord wood. The lean-to was attached to the far end of a corrugated metal shed that had sliding wood doors on both ends.

Dev trudged through the snow to the lean-to and stopped next to the wagon. Mr. Trent stopped his loading and looked at his family's guest.

"What happen, the girls run you out?" he asked. Mr. Trent was dressed in brown Carhartt bib overalls and a brown Carhartt coat, both stained and battered, giving evidence of long and frequent use. To cover his thinning hair, he wore a battered denim blue baseball cap with the logo from the local grain elevator on it. His weathered face was seamed, but Dev was glad to realize those were laugh lines around the mouth and eyes.

Dev smiled. "I was afraid if I hung around in there any longer, they'd dig up an apron for me and put me to work. Decided I'd be better off out here. Use a hand?"

"Sure. Help's always appreciated." Mr. Trent nodded his head toward the open door of the metal shed. "There's an extra pair of work gloves on the bench in there, if you want."

"I do," Dev replied. "My hands aren't toughened up enough for manual labor. Too much easy work on the computers."

Dev walked into the shed and was surprised to find the interior dominated by a large evaporator tank of the kind used to make maple syrup. At the front end of the building was a large metal storage tank for collecting sap. Tools were arranged neatly on the wooden bench. Scattered around the interior were some old wooden kitchen chairs, a couple of stools and even a battered captain's chair. In the other back corner was a mixed pile of oak chunks and soft wood for use in the firebox of the evaporator. An old AM/FM radio hung over the workbench. Looking at the workbench, he found a pair of leather work gloves and put them on as he went back outside.

"You make your own maple syrup?" he asked as he started loading wood into the wagon.

"Yup. Every spring. Gives me and Shane something to do.

Learned from my father-in-law. He was known far and wide for his maple syrup. Mother—my wife—takes ribbons at the county fair every year with her maple cream candy and such like. Recipes she got from her mother. It's a lot of work in a short period of time, but we enjoy it."

"Maybe I'll have to talk Nadine into bringing me up one of those weekends. Grandpa Walker used to have a bachelor brother who made his own syrup. Sometimes Dad and I would go out and help him."

Mr. Trent laughed. "Luck to you on that. Nadine usually likes to stay far away at syrup time. Since she's the oldest, she used to have to drive the tractor while we gathered sap."

Dev grinned at that. "Well then maybe Molly and I'll have to come up without her."

The two men worked steady at filling the wagon box with chunks of wood. They kept the pace slow, so as not to work up a sweat, and stopped occasionally for rest breaks. Then they would lean their arms on the sides of the wagon box, stare out at the snow and the wooded acres that surrounded the little farmstead, and talk. "We got all day to get this done," Mr. Trent had said. "No since killing ourselves at it."

"You split all this by hand, or do you use a splitter?" Dev asked as they loaded.

"I've got a splitter, of course, but I've also got a big old stump out back of the wood shed, and a double-bit axe, which I use sometimes." He then grinned. "Mother calls it my mad pile. It's a great way to work out frustrations."

Dev nodded. "There are times when I wish I had one of those at home. Usually I just end up going down to the campus and the gym, pound on the heavy bag, or work the speed bag."

Mr. Trent nodded. "Every man should have a mad pile of some kind."

It was turning into a beautiful winter morning. The snowstorm of the previous night was gone, replaced by sunshine, bright blue sky and a few puffs of clouds. The air was cold though, and the sun did little to warm the earth.

Once they had the wagon box full, Mr. Trent drove the tractor around to the side of the house, then opened a basement window and placed a metal chute from the wagon box through the window. The window opened into the furnace room of the basement, and the two men set to work tossing chunks of wood down the chute.

During one of the breaks Mr. Trent said, "So you're one of those English grad students like Nadine." It was and wasn't a question.

"Well, kind of," Dev hedged. "She's an English major. American romanticism. Hawthorne, Emerson, Melville. Those wacky New Englanders." Seeing the confused look on Mr. Trent's face, he explained in a little more detail. "It's a style of writing and a group of writers from the early part of the nineteenth century. *Moby Dick. The Scarlet Letter.*"

Mr. Trent nodded in recognition. "Okay, now I'm with you. Back in high school, American Literature wasn't one of my better subjects. I think it made Mrs. Granderson old before her time dragging me through my junior year."

Devlin smiled. "To be honest, I can't really see what Nadine finds so fascinating about that period myself. I like Henry Thoreau and some Poe, but the rest of that bunch are a little too stilted for my taste. Kind of like comparing an English mystery novel and an American detective story. Anyway, I'm not in the English department, exactly. I'm in the American Studies program. That's a fancy title for a multi-disciplined approach. Instead of studying a period of American literature, we take some aspect of American life or culture and study it from several directions." Devlin could see he was losing his audience again, so he added, "For example, my area of study is the Old West. I look at the literature, history, art, music, pop culture. In particular I'm studying the image of the Western in film and popular fiction."

Mr. Trent grinned. "Now where was that class when I was in high school? I could have done good in that. And you can actually get college credit for studying something like that?"

"Yeah, but it's not as easy as it sounds. My undergraduate degree is in journalism, so I had a good solid background in a variety of subjects, primarily literature and history. And my mother made sure I had a good upbringing in art and music. I was going to be a newspaper reporter, right up until my senior year. Then I took a history class on the American West to round out my schedule and I got hooked. That's when I found out about the whole American Studies thing. Next thing I knew, I was signed up for grad school."

"So that's how you met Nadine," Mr. Trent said.

"Well, yes and no. While I'm not 'in' the English department, I've taken a few lit classes, and I guess we'd seen each other around campus. A university is a big place, but when you get focused on one department, it gets real small, real fast. And of course we live in the same building. That's really where we met. We got to talking, found out we had some similar interests, and eventually became friends."

"I'm glad you did. I worry about her and Molly a lot, down there on their own. I've got to tell you, it's been a relief knowing she's got someone to help her out, especially with that car of hers."

Devlin laughed. "I can understand that. And I'm glad auto shop was one of my better classes in high school. It's come in real handy." Then he returned to throwing chunks of wood down the chute to the basement.

After they unloaded the wagon, Mr. Trent declared it was time for a coffee break, so he and Dev headed in through the back door to the utility room. Shane had just finished working over the driveway and joined them. The three men kicked off their boots and left them by the door so they wouldn't track slush through the house. Their coats went on hooks on the wall, and hats and gloves were dropped on the floor next to a heat duct to dry. With Mr. Trent in the lead, they trooped into the kitchen, poured their coffees and sat down at the kitchen table.

Mrs. Trent was working near the stove, pouring the vegetable soup from the night before into a crock pot. The breakfast dishes had been washed and put away, and the counters were clear for whatever cooking project might come up next.

Watching his wife with the soup, Mr. Trent said, "Looks like leftovers for lunch, boys."

Mrs. Trent turned toward them. "Yes, and you men are on your own as well. I'm putting the soup in the crock pot. There's lunch meat and cheese in the fridge, so you won't go hungry. Try not to dirty too many dishes."

"Where are you going?" Mr. Trent asked. As they were talking, Nadine, Verona and Molly came into the kitchen as well.

"I have to go down to Lansing to finish up some shopping, Dad," Nadine said. "Mom and Ronnie are going with me, but you boys are going to have to take care of Molly." Then she turned to Devlin. "That's if I can borrow your car."

He smiled and started to reach in his pocket for his wallet. "Okay, I guess. But you'll need to put gas in it."

She placed her hand on his shoulder. "I'll take care of it. You don't mind watching Molly, do you?"

"Course not." He picked Molly up and held her on his lap. "We'll have a great time here, won't we Sprout?" The little girl looked up at him, seriousness in her bright green eyes, so much like her mother's and grandmother's. "But I wanna go with Mom and Grandma and Aunt Ronnie," she said.

"Moll, they're just going to grown-up stores," he said. "You won't have any fun with them. But we're going to build a snowman right out there in the front yard, and I heard your Uncle Shane say he might be able to come up with some sleds and saucers to play on the hill."

She swung around on Devlin's lap to look at Shane. "Really?"

Trying to suppress a grin, the young man said, "I just might, if there was going to be anyone around to play on the hill with."

Molly turned back to her mother. "Okay, I'll stay."

Nadine sat alone at a table in the crowded food court area of the mall. She had managed to secure a small table with four chairs, and she had quickly filled the chairs with packages. The noise level in the food court was deafening, and the mall itself was far more crowded than even she had anticipated. Yet still she was satisfied. She had been able to pick up the last couple of presents she needed for Molly, and that made the whole experience worthwhile.

As she sat there, drinking a cup of coffee and eating a cinnamon roll, she watched the ebb and flow of the crowd and realized she really was seeing a cross-section of humanity—young and old, rich, poor and in-between, all sorts of ethnic groups. Oddly enough there were very few children. Then she noticed her sister searching the crowd for her, so she stood up and waved.

Verona came over, laid her package from the bookstore down on the table, then pointed at the cinnamon roll and said, "I need one of those and some coffee."

Nadine watched as her sister went over to the Cinnabon counter and stood in line. For the umpteenth time that day she reminded herself that a mall two days before Christmas was no place to be if you didn't like to stand in line, and admitted this probably wasn't one of her better ideas. But it had been necessary. Mind-numbing Christmas music continued to drone from the strategically placed loud speakers in the ceiling and for the most part she had been able to tune it out.

Soon her younger sister was back with a large coffee and a gooey cinnamon roll. As Verona sat down, Nadine asked, "What'd you do with Mother?"

"I left her in the book store. She was looking at books on tractors, for dad. Does it bother you that we're supposed to be vital young women in our twenties and Mom's twice as old and still out-shopping us?"

Nadine smiled and shook her head. "Dad always said Mom was a marathon shopper. I'm just out of shape. I don't do it enough. I spend all my time in classes or grading papers."

"Well you're not in classes or grading papers this week," Verona replied. "Are you going to cut loose and have a little fun?"

"I thought that's what I've been doing."

"You know what I mean."

Nadine blushed and took a sip of coffee. "Verona Renae!"

"I'm just saying, if I had a guy like Dev on the string, I sure wouldn't be wasting him. Have you two even had a sleep-over?"

"Well, he has fallen asleep a couple of times on my couch. And for the hundredth times, we're just friends. Besides, I have a responsibility to my daughter. I can't just go running around having flings."

"Who said anything about having flings? I'm just wondering why a reasonably attractive young woman like yourself hasn't gone out on a date with a devilishly handsome young man who seems to adore her and her daughter."

"Verona, drop it, okay?"

Verona just shook her head at that. "Okay. So are you and your just friend going to Christina's party tonight?"

"We've talked about it. Dev said he'd go."

"That's a start. Now when mom gets here, you and I are heading down to a little dress store where I saw the perfect party dress for you."

"Ronnie, I've already got a party dress. I don't need another one."

"Nadine, I know you. What you've got is a cute little young-mother type party dress. What you need is a vibrant young college co-ed party dress. Trust me. You wear this dress for an evening, and Dev will want to be more than just friends."

Nadine shook her head. "You're incorrigible."

Verona smiled back at her with that luminous Trent smile. I know. It's one of my more endearing qualities."

That evening, Dev Walker found himself seated at a table in a large rental hall, nursing a plastic Christmas cup of punch and wondering what he'd gotten himself into. It had sounded innocent enough at first blush—a cousin's annual Christmas party for family and friends. He was not expecting a rental hall decorated with artificial pine boughs, multi-colored miniature lights, and all the bells and wreaths one could expect. Each long table had a paper Christmas tablecloth and a centerpiece. At the front end of the hall, where the kitchen was, a potluck buffet spread had been put out, with enough food to feed a crowd twice this size—sliced ham and turkey, cheeses, hot dishes, salads and desserts. At the back end of the hall, on a slightly raised platform, another of Nadine's cousins had set up his DJ equipment and had been cranking out mostly Christmas music with a few dance tunes mixed in. The tables were set up along the side walls, leaving a nice wide aisle. And in front of the stage area, a large space had been cleared for a dance floor.

His mother would have found the whole event exceedingly tasteless, even tacky. Which was probably why he was finding the whole evening so fascinating. It was the kind of party his Walker relatives would have thrown, and when it came down to it, he was more Walker than anything else.

Of course the introductions to cousins, neighbors and childhood friends had all been a blur. For the first dozen he had tried to keep them straight, then quickly gave up. He was known around campus for his quick grasp of his students' names and faces, but this was a task too daunting even for him. Supper had been served shortly after their arrival, and then most of the food had stayed out on the tables for grazing. Dancing and talking had followed, and he had danced a couple of times with Nadine, and a couple of times with Verona, even though her boyfriend was present. But mostly he sat at his table with his punch, and watched all the holiday activities.

He had been surprised when Nadine came down stairs in

the blue sequined party dress. The bodice fit tight and the skirt hung to just above the knees. She had styled her dark hair up on her head. Her heels gave a bounce to her walk and for a moment he was quite speechless. He discovered she had the same effect on the crowd at the party when they arrived. Once the dancing had started, she and Verona had spent most of their time on the dance floor. Currently the sisters were swishing their skirts and vamping to an up-tempo version of *Santa Baby*. He shook his head and smiled.

For himself, he was casually attired in a black Dockers and a gray ski sweater. He could have easily found himself up with the dancers, but this was Nadine's family and friends and he was content to stay on the sidelines and let her shine. Being at the front of group was nothing new to him, and Nadine frequently said he could make himself at home anywhere.

In the periphery of his vision he noticed Verona's boyfriend sit down in the folding metal chair next to him.

Dev looked over at the younger man, a rail-thin specimen with unruly dark hair named Curt Larrand. "Those Trent girls really light up a room, don't they?" Dev said to his counterpart.

Curt nodded. "It's good to see Nadine cut loose and have fun again. She's been so controlled for so long, I'd almost forgotten how much like Ronnie she used to be."

"You've known them for awhile then?" Dev asked.

"Yep. Verona and I grew up together. You know how it is out here in these rural communities. You know everybody, even if you're not related to them. We didn't start dating until we got in college, though. But I've been coming to these parties, and others, since I was in high school. I've gotta tell you, growing up, we all thought Nadine was hot."

"That's hard to imagine. I've only known the controlled Nadine. Most of the people in the English department don't even really notice her. Let alone think of her as hot."

"It's a shame that good-for-nothing jerk treated her that way. Leaving her with the kid was bad enough, but that's not that big a deal anymore. The rotten part was how deeply he hurt the fun-loving Nadine. It's like she's afraid to let it happen again, so she's buried that part of her down deep. Then that big fight she had with her dad didn't help. It was a long time before she came home again."

"I know a little about that," Dev said. "She's told me about it. And other things." He shook his head. "I wish I could have known her before."

"Maybe you can coax that Nadine back out," Curt replied. "You've had a good effect on her so far."

Before he could comment further, Dev noticed Nadine and Verona coming toward them. When the sisters were close enough to overhear, he said, "Curt, I think we're in trouble."

The sisters came down the other side of the table. Nadine leaned across the table on her forearms, showing a respectable amount of cleavage. "C'mon professor-boy, I need someone to dance with."

Dev laughed and looked at Curt. "Told you."

🎁

The first song had been a contemporary pop Christmas song. After it was over he expected her to turn him loose, but the DJ segued into Dean Martin's *Baby, It's Cold Outside* and she slid in close with his right arm around her waist and her right hand in his left pressed against his chest. He looked down into her sparkling green eyes. Slowly, the people, the dance floor and the hall faded into the background until he was hardly even aware of his surroundings. Softly, he sang along to the song, and Nadine smiled back at him with her luminous smile.

"I've always liked this song," she said.

"Me too. Especially this version."

"Oh yes."

The music shifted to Nat King Cole singing *The Christmas Song*. Nadine snuggled closer and put both arms around his neck. He put his arms around her waist. They barely swayed to the music, not really dancing, content to be in each other's arms. He found himself drawn into those green eyes. He bent his head so they could touch cheeks. Softly, they brushed lips, then returned for a more lingering kiss, then another. No thrusting passion, but a soft melding of two souls.

As the song ended, they pulled away, and she waved her hand in front of her face, fanning herself.

"Woo. I think I need to sit down."

He let her lead him back to their table. Thankfully, he noticed the crowd was pointedly ignoring them. For once he found himself uncomfortable at the forefront.

They sat down and he took a quick drink of punch.

"I'm sorry," she said. "I don't know what came over me."

"Good music and the holiday season," he said.

"Yes, that's got to be it." She took a drink from her punch glass. "I hope this evening hasn't been too dreadful for you. I know how hard it is to have fun at a party where you don't really know anyone."

He smiled. "You know me. I'm never a stranger for long wherever I go."

They continued to sit there and make small talk and before his eyes he saw the fun Nadine fade back into that dark, deeply-buried closet and close the door. In her place was the quiet, sometimes sad Nadine he knew so well. He also knew, though, that their relationship would never be the same.

THREE

Saturday, December 24

"Idiot!" he hissed as the blade of the ax descended on the chunk of wood. And he repeated the word with each swing of the ax as he worked his way through Mr. Trent's mad pile—place a chunk on the big log, swing the ax, sweep the pieces aside, reposition the biggest remaining piece and swing again. He had developed a rhythm, slow and methodical, not working up a sweat.

Dev Walker had spent a troubled night. The ride home from the party was quiet, and when they reached the Trent house, Nadine had gone on up to bed. Dev made up the sofa sleeper and got into his sweats, but sleep wouldn't come and he found it difficult to concentrate on his book. His mind had kept returning to the events of the party and the glimpse he had had of a different side of his friend. And he thought about what it all meant to their relationship. But mostly he thought about how stupid he'd been.

"Idiot," he hissed again as he continued his cathartic rhythm—set, swing, clear, repeat.

He didn't know how long he been working at the mad pile when he finally stopped for a break. Dev didn't want to work up a sweat, or get over-tired and limit his body's defenses in the cold. With a solid chunk he buried the head of the ax into the top of the base stump.

"Hope you weren't fixing on cutting through the whole pile," said a voice behind him. "I wasn't figuring on bringing up another load until after Christmas."

Startled, Dev turned around, facing back toward the other sheds, the driveway, the house, and Mr. Trent. He stared at the older man for a minute, then gave a little half grin. "Sorry. I got into a rhythm you know. Guess I had some things to think over."

Mr. Trent walked over and started stacking up some of the loose chunks Dev had created. "I know how that goes. Done it a time or two myself. I expect you're thinking about last night."

"You heard, huh? I guess I'd better go get my things packed and hit the road."

Mr. Trent stopped stacking and looked at Dev. "Why? You leaving?"

"You tell me. I figured this was the scene where you run me off your property like a stray dog."

"Well, I thought about it. But on Christmas Eve? I do that and then I'll have to face that house full of womenfolk. Nope. Not doing that. Not over a kiss."

Dev shook his head. "It was more than a kiss. I broke the rules. If I was in your shoes, I'd sure run me off."

"Good thing you're not me, then. Dev, I'm just a simple country boy. I don't begin to understand this complicated relationship you have with my daughter. Makes my head hurt just trying to sort it out. Reminds me of some of those stories Mother watches on TV. But I'm a pretty good judge of people, and I like what I've seen of you so far. I don't think you're the type to take advantage."

"You don't understand, Mr. Trent. Nadine and I had an arrangement. No romance. That's the way she wanted it from the very beginning, and I agreed to that."

"Son, I don't know if you've noticed or not, but people have a way of changing over time. Now I don't know what you two may or may not have been feeling last night. I just know that with you in her life, my daughter's happier than she's been since before Molly was born. She's almost like she used to be. And of course I don't know whether you've changed or not, but I think you're good for each other, and I'd hate to see anything mess that up." Then he stopped talking and shrugged. "But what do I know? I married the only woman I ever fell in love with, just as quickly as she'd have me."

With that, Mr. Trent left him, heading back toward the metal syrup-making shed. Dev Walker watched him leave, then turned to the task of stacking the remaining wood chunks. Was it really that simple? He thought of his own parents' relationship—marriage and divorce. And their relationships without each other. What exactly did he feel for Nadine?

As if summoned by the thought, he heard snow crunching under someone's feet and looked up to see Nadine coming toward him. She was looking very much the farm girl—multi-colored knit cap, brown Carhartt jacket, faded jeans tucked into snowmobile boots. In each hand she carried a travel mug with steam issuing from the top. As she approached, she held out one mug for him.

"I know you usually drink it black, but Mom had some of that peppermint mocha creamer you like, so I added it."

"Thanks," he replied.

Indicating the wood pile, she said, "Looks like you've been busy."

"Idle hands, you know. I'm not used to this much inactivity."

"I know." She took a sip of coffee. "I saw Dad out here talking with you. What did he want?"

"He told me to go easy on his mad pile because he didn't want to haul any more up before tomorrow. I thought this was his wood shed."

Nadine shook her head. "Yes and no. He has another shed back in the woods for the fresh cut stuff. Don't ask me why he does it that way."

"If you're dad's anything like my dad's family, he probably

learned it from his grandfather. One of those unwritten family traditions."

She nodded. "That's probably it." Nadine then took a deep breath, steeled herself, and looked up at Dev. "I've been doing a lot of thinking. You know. About last night."

"Yeah, I've been doing some of that myself."

"I don't know what came over me. It must have been too much holiday spirit. The party. The music. Christmas."

He smiled. "I'm sure all of it had an effect."

"Anyway, I just wanted to say I'm sorry. You know. For the kiss. I shouldn't have done that."

"I'm just as much to blame."

"So I was thinking, maybe we should just pretend it didn't really happen."

"Just a kind of holiday kiss under the mistletoe, and just let it go at that?"

"Exactly. Two close friends sharing a Christmas kiss. Nothing more than that."

Dev looked down into her moist green eyes, down to their depths, searching for the thoughts behind them. "Are you sure that's how you want it?"

"I'm sure."

He nodded once, almost as much to himself as to her. "Okay." He drank some of the coffee, then handed the mug back to her. "Listen, while I was out here working this morning, I remembered an errand I need to run before tonight. Make my apologies to your family for me, all right?"

"Will you be back in time for supper? Molly will be heartbroken if you're not there."

"I don't know. I hope so. I'll do the best I can."

He left her standing by the mad pile, her thoughts as gray as the leaden winter sky above her.

■

Nadine sat on the sofa in the living room, her legs tucked up under her, Dev's book unopened in her lap. Molly sat beside her, watching a Christmas cartoon on the TV. Across the room,

Verona sat in their mother's easy chair, a folding table in front of her, wrapping anonymous boxes in Christmas paper, bows and ribbon, and occasionally throwing a glance at the TV.

Nadine couldn't believe how much had changed in such a short period of time. Yesterday had been one of the happiest she'd spent in a long time. In fact the whole trip had been shaping up to be one of her best Christmases ever. Until that kiss. That simple, stupid kiss. But was it wrong? It hadn't felt wrong in the moment, only after, when she realized what had happened. Now she wasn't sure what was right or what she wanted. She only knew she felt like something bright had gone out of her life, and she was afraid she'd never get it back.

"Nadine Eliza Trent, are you listening to me?"

Nadine shook her head to clear it of fog and looked up to see her mother standing in the living room doorway, a red and green Christmas apron over her gray knit top and black knit pants.

"I'm sorry, Mom. What did you want?"

"I need you to help me get supper on."

Nadine put the book aside, stood up and followed her mother into the kitchen. From the pantry she took another Christmas apron, this one with a holly pattern, and put it on over her green sweatshirt with the snowman scene and her jeans. "What do you want me to do?'

Mrs. Trent stood at the stove, a wood spoon in her hand. She pointed at the end of the kitchen table with the spoon, where a large boneless ham waited on a cutting board. "You get the ham ready while I finish this batch of fudge."

"Okay, Mom." Nadine sat down at the table and began scoring the ham in the perfect diamond pattern her mother had taught her back when she was in high school. How many such hams had she prepared in the years since? It was almost second nature. She cut the ham, then opened up the plastic jar of whole cloves her mother had out ready on the table. As she pushed cloves into the diamonds formed on the ham, she remembered the last candied ham she had made. It was a special Sunday dinner for her and Molly and Dev. Dev had spent the weekend working on her beat-up car, trying to get it back into usable shape yet again. She had fixed candied ham, scalloped potatoes, oven-baked macaroni and cheese, a salad and homemade rolls. After dinner they had watched football, and then a movie after Molly had gone to bed, and fell asleep on the couch. And it had been one of her best weekends of the fall.

"What's that smile about?"

Nadine looked up to see her mother watching her. She shook her head, then said, "Just remembering the last time I made a candied ham. Dev couldn't get enough. It's his favorite."

"Then I hope he makes it back in time for supper tonight."

Nadine felt the grayness envelope her again. "He won't. He won't be back until next week when it's time to go home."

Mrs. Trent pulled out a chair, sat down at the table and started helping her daughter with the cloves. "That sounds like something you want to talk about."

"Want to talk about? No. Need to talk about? Yes, I guess I do." Nadine quietly worked on the cloves for a few moments, then said, "I messed up, Mom. I ruined everything."

"And how did you do that?"

"Dev and I had an agreement, back at the very beginning. No romance. We were just going to be friends." She held up her hand to stop her mother from interrupting. "I know. I know. It's not that simple. But I thought that's what I wanted. I knew I had to look out for Molly, and I knew I couldn't take care of her and have any romantic entanglements in my life. We were still on our own back then, remember?"

"I remember." After a moment or two of silence, she said, "And maybe it was a way to keep from getting hurt again?"

"Oh, I think that was probably a given, although I didn't realize it at the time. I was scared, Mom. I'll admit it. My track record with men wasn't too good at that point. So when I met Dev, I laid out the ground rules right from the start. And he agreed and life was good. I had a friend, someone to depend on. And I wasn't alone anymore. And I didn't have to worry about the whole romance aspect."

"Until last night when you kissed on the dance floor."

"Or maybe before then and we just didn't know it. But the kiss was what did it. It changed everything. And then I did something even dumber. This morning, I told Dev I wanted to go on as if the kiss never happened."

"What did he say to that?"

"He agreed. And then he told me about this errand he had just remembered. I'm not that stupid. Funny. All this time, and I never wondered why Dev agreed to our original arrangement. But I've been thinking about it a lot since this morning. I've been acting all along like I'm this irresistible force to men. Maybe he never really was ever interested in me as anything more than a friend."

"And maybe you're just butt-blind."

Nadine looked up to see Verona standing in the doorway to the kitchen. "Excuse me?"

"Well you must be butt-blind not to see how much in love he is with you and your daughter. Anybody with two eyes and a brain can see he's completely devoted to you two. Except you."

"What are you talking about?"

Verona walked over and sat down at the table as well. "Nadine, you're my big sister and you know I love you to pieces, but my God are you dense! You've told me about some of the things the three of you do together. How much time you spend together. I know married couples who don't spend that much time together. And who aren't as happy. But you don't have to look any farther than coming up here this weekend. How many guys would drive two hours into mid-Michigan to spend Christmas with a group of strangers, just so a friend could be with her family? Most guys would have dropped you off and headed on up to Traverse City or Boyne for some skiing. Actually most guys wouldn't be spending time around a single mother in the first place."

"Mom insisted he stay."

"Sis, I don't know how to break it to you, but Mom's influence generally doesn't extend beyond Dad and us kids. Total strangers don't usually feel obligated to follow her wishes."

"Curt does."

Verona shook her head in disgust. "Boyfriend! Hello! Tell her, Mom."

Nadine looked to her mother. Mrs. Trent had a hand in front of her mouth, and Nadine thought she could almost see a smirk on her lips. "Much as it pains me to admit it, Ronnie's right. I'm sorry."

"So what do I do?"

"I guess that depends on what you want to do," Mrs. Trent replied.

"I don't want to lose him. I can't imagine not having Dev in our lives. And Molly would be just as heartbroken."

"Then I guess you're going to have to throw out your little set of relationship rules you two cooked up," Verona said.

"But what if he doesn't come back?"

Mrs. Trent smiled. "He'll be back. And we'd better get back to getting supper ready or there won't be anything to eat when he does."

"But Mom, I told you he won't be back today."

"Spend Christmas without his two favorite girls? No honey, he'll be back. So you'd better get your game plan set."

Christmas Eve supper in the Trent household had developed into a tradition. In the early years, when Nadine and Verona were still little, supper had been a simple affair. But as the girls got older, Mrs. Trent turned it into the family's formal holiday meal. Mrs. Trent's family gathered for a big potluck dinner on Christmas Day, so Christmas Eve was the time to be spent with the immediate family. Guests were not unusual, and this Christmas was no exception. Verona's boyfriend, Curt, came over, and Shane's current girlfriend, a petite quiet blonde named Meghan McQuade, in her first formal dinner with the family. And true to Mrs. Trent's prediction, Devlin Walker arrived barely an hour before mealtime offering apologies for being gone all day, but no explanations for where he had been.

The meal was a tense one for Nadine. There had been no time for talking when Dev returned as she had been busy helping her mother get supper on the table. And there was no chance to pull him aside for a talk during supper. But Molly was delighted to have Dev back, and insisted on him sitting between her and her mother for supper.

After supper, Nadine and Verona helped their mother clear up, put the dishes in the dishwater, and return the kitchen back to normal, while the rest of the family went out to sled on the bowl-shaped hill on the back side of the house. Once the dishes were in the dishwasher, Verona also went out to the sledding hill, but Nadine stayed and washed up the pans they didn't want to put in the machine.

Eventually, with the kitchen back to normal, Nadine went outside and found her father standing at the top of the hill, back by the house, watching Verona and Curt, Shane and Meghan, and Dev and Molly having fun. The Trents had a variety of sledding equipment collected over the years, from metal-runner sleds and wooden toboggans to hard plastic saucers and shaped craft and plastic toboggans. The sledders were trying them all. Shane would show off for Meghan on his snowboard, and usually managed to take a fall before he got to the bottom of the hill. Verona and Curt preferred snuggling up on a wooden toboggan. Sometimes Dev and Molly would fold themselves up on a saucer, but usually he sent her down on a plastic toboggan while he shadowed her with a sled. The mercury light by the house, and the one back by the outbuildings provided enough illumination for them to see.

Nadine walked through the snow to stand next to her father. Flurries were falling, sparkling in the crisp night air. Nadine was dressed in jeans, her Carharrt jacket and stocking cap.

Putting her arm through his, she leaned against her father.

Smiling, he looked down at her. "Kitchen's back to normal, huh?"

"Finally. I swear Mom feels it's her duty to dirty every dish in the house when she puts on one of her suppers. I'm sure glad you bought her that dishwasher."

"Me too. With you girls gone off to college, Shane and I have to do the clean-up. So is you're mother coming out to join us?"

"On Christmas Eve? You know better. She has way too much to do to get things ready. And she doesn't want any help. I was essentially shooed out of the house."

Mr. Trent shook his head. "She does love her holidays. Especially Christmas. And she's really enjoying this year with all of you kids home."

"I can tell. And it looks like everyone's having a good time out here, too."

"Why don't you go join them. I think Molly would like that."

"I know she would." She pulled her arm out of his and walked away a couple of steps before turning back to her father. "What do you think of him, Dad?"

"I like what I've seen so far, but I've only just met him. He seems devoted to the two of you, and he's willing to spend Christmas with your family. Not many would do that."

"Thanks, Dad."

🎁

Dev Walker stood in the front yard, near the end of the driveway, looking off to the south of the ridge where the land opened up into farms. Mercury lights and Christmas lights dotted the landscape around the scattered houses, and the dirt roads broke up the snow-covered fields like a downy patchwork quilt. He knew each cluster of lights represented a family gathered together to enjoy this special holiday time. How long had it been since he'd had that kind of Christmas? Had there ever been a time like that? The light flurries persisted, the crystals catching what light was available. He found the view incredibly beautiful, and was glad he had the opportunity to see it. This was all so different than what he was used to in the city. He thought of those families, nestled in for the night, not worrying about the snow or bad roads. Just happy to be together on this special night. Sitting around the table playing games, laughing, talking. Or maybe off in groups of two or three wrapping up last minute gifts or making plans for something special. All oblivious to the rest of the world.

Behind him, he heard the crunching of someone walking through the snow of the driveway. He could tell by the sound that it was Mr. Trent. In the short time he'd been around the family, he had learned the older man's tread.

"Watching for Santa Claus?" Mr. Trent asked him.

Dev smiled and said, "No sign of him yet, but it's early." He paused, then turned to look at the older man. "You're a lucky man, Mr. Trent. A warm, loving family, a nice little homestead, and some fabulous views. But you don't need me to tell you that."

"Well, I consider myself lucky, but I'm glad to know you think so too. Kind of surprised to hear a city boy admiring all this country living."

Dev looked at him. "Comes as a bit of a surprise to me, too. I guess I'm more my father's son than I thought. I consider myself fortunate to be able spend this holiday with your family. It means more to me than you'll ever know."

"That sure sounds like a man with a lot on his mind." He paused for a moment, staring out across the fields. "Dev, are things going to be okay between you and Nadine?"

The young man shrugged. "I hope so. We'll have to see."

"Anything I can do to help?"

Dev smiled again at him. "Just keep your fingers crossed and think good thoughts. Maybe I haven't messed this all up yet."

OUR

Sunday, December 25

The house was quiet as Devlin Walker sat on the sofa bed, reading *A Christmas Carol*. The last of the three spirits had departed and Scrooge had awakened to a bright, cheerful Christmas Day, just as he did every year when Dev read the story. The lamp was on next to the sofa where Dev was reading, and the lights of the Christmas tree and the multi-color lights in the windows were still plugged in. Ever since he was a kid, Dev had enjoyed having the tree lights on. He remembered sneaking from his bedroom down to the living room in the early morning hours, hoping to catch Santa Claus, but only finding the toys and stocking the Christmas elf had left behind.

As if on cue, he heard footsteps on the stairs, but quickly recognized them as Nadine's. She came into the room, wearing a flannel nightgown, her arms full of packages, her dark hair hanging loose around her face.

"I knew I'd find you awake."

He looked over at his watch on the end table next to the lamp. It was a little after 1 AM. "You know me too well. I've never been able to sleep on Christmas Eve."

"That will come in handy. Want to help me set up Molly's Santa gifts?"

Devlin closed the book and stood up from the sofa. "Sure.

Where do we start?"

"Take this Barbie® apartment and get it set up. I'll work on the baby doll and high chair."

Devlin took the box from her, then sat down cross-legged on the floor to open it up. He gave the instructions a quick glance and decided it would be simple enough, so he dumped out the pieces and started organizing them. Nadine was doing the same with the high chair.

They worked quietly for awhile before Nadine asked, "So did you get all your errands done today?"

"I think so. Sorry I ran out on you like that. I hope your mother wasn't too upset."

Nadine shook her head. "No, Mother was fine. So what did you do?"

"I did some driving. Made some phone calls. Dad and Steph say 'Merry Christmas' by the way."

"You called your Dad?"

"Yeah, I wanted to wish him a Merry Christmas. And I had some things I needed to talk over with him."

"Like what?"

"Oh, just things."

"You're being very cryptic."

He smiled at her. "Am I?" He looked at her sitting on the sofa bed, the high chair forgotten in her lap. He noticed her white flannel gown had little poinsettias in patterns across it, and how they brought out the green in her eyes. And her dark hair framed her oval face with its pert nose and cherry red lips waiting to be kissed.

"Yes, you are," she said, but the corners of her mouth wrinkled up and he knew she wasn't upset with him.

"Do you remember the first time we met?" he asked.

Puzzlement came over her face. "It was when you moved into the upstairs apartment. Are you trying to change the subject?"

"You and Molly were sitting on that wide cement railing of the steps, eating popsicles. You had on your khaki shorts and that red top with the spaghetti straps. Your hair was pulled back in a ponytail. Molly wore a yellow sundress. It was hotter than Hades and I was lugging boxes up three flights of stairs. On one of my trips through you offered me a glass of iced tea. I thought you were very attractive, and I enjoyed talking to you."

"I enjoyed talking to you, too. And I thought you were cute, or I wouldn't have offered you the ice tea. But what's that have to do with today?"

"I don't know. Just got to thinking about it, I guess."

"Dev, in all the time we've known each other, you never asked me out. Why?"

He shrugged. "I guess I never got the chance. We decided pretty early on that we would just be friends, remember?"

"I remember, but you agreed. Why?"

"Does it matter? It's ancient history."

"I think it's important. We shouldn't keep secrets from each other."

"I guess I was a little shy when it came to relationships."

She shook her head. "You? Shy? Never in all the time I've known you. You've had lots of relationships."

"Not serious ones. I was always afraid of getting in too deep. After watching my parents all through my childhood, I figured any relationship I got into wouldn't last, so why go through all the heartache."

"So is that what you and Sara fought about?"

Devlin shook his head. "No. Oddly enough, we fought about you. Sara said she couldn't compete with you anymore, that it was so obvious that you and I were in love that she didn't stand a chance in the relationship. I told her she was crazy, but she left anyway."

"Well aren't we a fine pair? Two lonely people afraid to take a chance on happiness."

"Or maybe we've already found it and are too blind to see."

"Ronnie said mostly the same thing this afternoon. Basically she said we need to wake up and admit how we feel about each other."

"And what did you say to that?"

"Well, I predicted you wouldn't be back tonight. Why did you come back, anyway?"

"I had a special Christmas present I wanted to give you." He leaned forward and felt around among the wrapped presents under the tree. After a few moments, he brought out a small, square package wrapped in red paper with gold ribbon and bow holding it closed.

When she saw the shape of the package Nadine said, "Dev, you didn't."

"I don't know if I'm any good in a serious, long-term relationship, but I do know I don't want a life without you and Molly in it." He handed her the package.

"Dev ..." she started to say.

"Like I said, I want you and Molly in my life, but I'm not living a lie, pretending I don't feel what I do. I love you, Nadine, and I love your daughter. Took me awhile to realize that. Maybe that was for the best. Now it's up to you."

Nadine was silent, holding the box in her lap. Then she said, "I did some thinking today, too. When you left, I was scared to death you wouldn't come back, and I realized, I don't want a life without you in it, either. I've been hiding behind motherhood so I wouldn't have to take a chance on getting hurt. It's funny how life makes other plans." She took the ring out of the box and held it out for him to put it on her finger. "The answer is yes."

🎁

Molly Trent woke up alone in the bed she had been sharing with her mother. She lay there for a few moments, listening for the sounds of reindeer hooves on the roof, or voices in one of the other rooms. But all she could hear were the normal quiet creaks and groans of the farmhouse, so she rolled over in the bed and looked at the digital clock on the bedside stand. The numbers read 4:52, and that meant everyone would be asleep for awhile longer.

Quietly, Molly got out of bed, put on her robe and stuck her feet into her slippers before easing out of the bedroom and down the hall to the stairway. She waited a moment at the top of the stairs, listening, but the house remained quiet. She started down the stairs, one at a time, leaning against the wall to avoid the squeaky parts of the steps. Before she was halfway down, Molly realized the lights from the Christmas tree were still blinking, and she hurried a little to get downstairs. Maybe Santa was still in the house.

As she neared the bottom, she looked through the banister and was disappointed to find no one in the living room. She continued down the stairs, and at the bottom turned into the room. First she glanced to the sofa sleeper to make sure Uncle Dev was still asleep, but what she saw made her smile. Uncle Dev was asleep, but next to him was her mother, her back to his chest and his arm over her waist. Then Molly looked to the Christmas tree and saw the new Barbie® and her apartment, and a baby doll in a high chair.

Careful not to make any sound, Molly tiptoed over to the Christmas tree and picked up her baby doll. Then she went to the sofa sleeper and carefully crawled in under the covers next to her mother. Molly knew this was going to be the best Christmas ever, because she had the one present she truly wanted—her mom, Uncle Dev and herself as a family. Lying next to her mother, she hugged her baby doll, listened to the sound of the two adults breathing, and watched the Christmas tree lights blink. Soon she was back to sleep and dreaming of Christmas day.

🎁 🎁 🎁

Keith Salisbury

Photo courtesy of Hillary Gregoire

Keith Salisbury has been a professional journalist working at weekly newspapers for 24 years. He currently serves as editor/photographer of a 17,000 free circulation weekly. An avid reader, he has also been an aspiring fiction writer since college. He and his wife live in rural mid-Michigan with their five house rabbits.